THE HUNTER
SOUTHEAST ASIA

THE HUNTER
SOUTHEAST ASIA

BRAD BAGWELL

Copyright © 2020 by Brad Bagwell.

All rights reserved. No part of this publication may be reproduced, distributed, or transmitted in any form or by any means, including photocopying, recording, or other electronic or mechanical methods, without the prior written permission of the publisher, except in the case of brief quotations embodied in critical reviews and certain other noncommercial uses permitted by copyright law. For permission requests, write to the publisher, addressed "Attention: Permissions Coordinator," at the address below.

Author Reputation Press LLC
45 Dan Road Suite 36
Canton MA 02021
www.authorreputationpress.com
Hotline: 1(800) 220-7660
Fax: 1(855) 752-6001

Ordering Information:
Quantity sales. Special discounts are available on quantity purchases by corporations, associations, and others. For details, contact the publisher at the address above.

Printed in the United States of America.

ISBN-13:   Softcover   978-1-952250-24-8
           Hardback   978-1-952250-26-2
           eBook   978-1-952250-25-5

Library of Congress Control Number: 2020905346

CHAPTER 1

WHAT ON EARTH AM I doing here? It seems like minute ago, I was standing in front of the lower level entrance to Lucky Plaza on Orchard Road in Singapore, getting ready to look for some cheap watches or one more suitcase that I really didn't need, but just couldn't seem to walk away from, and now I'm picking myself up in a remote spot on Sentosa Island.

They say Singapore is a fine city. There's a joke about that, since Singapore seems to have a fine for just about anything. A $200 fine for not flushing a public toilet, for example. But Singapore really is a great place. It is normally a very safe place, too. So, how did I get from a shopping center on Orchard Road, a place with a lot of people around, to this isolated area on Sentosa Island, 10 KM from where I last remember being?

As I begin to gather my senses, which some people say might be impossible for me, I realize how much time has passed as well! Now I'm really confused. What's happened to me in the last few days? Where have I been and what have I done? Where do I go to start getting some answers? As my thoughts continue to come together, I'm starting to get flashes of images that are letting me know I've had a very interesting time.

So, let's go back to Lucky Plaza. Where was I when I was getting ready to go there? I had to have been going there from the MRT Station across the street, through the tunnel under Orchard Road. There would have been too many people around if I'd been going in at the street entrance. What happened? Then I got one of those flashes! I vaguely remember that sting in my neck, seeing all the advertising posters lining the tunnel suddenly going gray. Then black.

As I start to concentrate on that flash, some of the other events of the past few days start coming into focus, too. But I can't get too far ahead or things will get jumbled. I've got to stay focused on one thing at a time. I've got to keep things straight or they won't make sense. Not like they're making any sense now, but I know it won't get better if I don't try to keep everything in order.

I had a room at the Hilton International on Orchard Road. I wonder if my stuff is still there? I know I wasn't scheduled to check out until the middle of next week, so it should be. I know I need to get there and check it out, since the clothes I have on now aren't in the best of shape. The next question is, do I have any money? Fortunately, there's about twenty Singapore dollars in my front pocket and my wallet with some credit cards in my back pocket. Until I figure out what happened and why, I don't think I want to use a credit card for anything. I'm not sure who did what to me and I don't want them to be able to trace me by my credit card use.

Why on earth did I think about that? And why would I worry about it? That was strange! Anyway, I guess I'd better be careful going back to the Hilton. There might be someone waiting for me there. I'm not sure who or why, but I'm beginning to get this tingling feeling that I have a second life that I live, that someone else seems to control. My "spidey senses" are starting to really get going.

Dusting myself off as best I can, I walk to the taxi stand and get into a cab. On the 15-minute ride to the Hilton, I keep trying to figure out what all these flash memories are. Trying to keep them in order the best I can. It's hard to do when you really have no clue what any of them really are or how they fit together. But I've got to keep trying.

As I enter the Hilton, the lobby bar in front of me is busy with the normal level of people. I remember a past trip here where there was a new girl whose nametag simply said "TRAINEE". We had a lot of fun with that, since we ended up calling her Tray Nee, kind of a Chinese sounding name. But that was a long time ago and I need to focus. As I turn to the right to get to the Registration Desk, my spidey senses are starting to warn me. There's nothing I can see that is cause for immediate concern, but I know I've got to keep paying attention to those spidey senses. I know they've saved me in the past.

That's another weird feeling. How and when did they save me in the past? And what did they save me from? This is really getting strange. Anyway, as I get to the Registration Desk, the girl behind the Desk hands me my room key. That's something that's always amazed me about some of the hotels in Asia. The people working there always seem to remember the guests and what room they're in. Yeah, I know, here comes a memory from when I was in Seoul, on my first trip to Asia.

Seems I spent a few days at the Sheraton Walker Hill before having to go to Pusan for a couple days. When I got back, the girl at the Registration Desk simply said, "Here's your key. I put you in the same room you were in last week." Needless to say, I was amazed that she could remember people and what room they were in. Maybe it was just me she remembered. Nah, I'm not that good looking. Well, maybe!

Back to the Hilton in Singapore and trying to figure out what I've been up to. Hopefully I was doing something good. Or at least something not too bad. I couldn't wait to get to my room and take a nice hot shower and get into some clean clothes. Even I was beginning to smell myself, so I knew the people around me weren't too thrilled.

I ended up in an elevator by myself, even though people were waiting. Guess I really didn't smell too good.

When I opened the door to my room, more of those weird flashes started popping into my head. I still had to keep them in focus and try to keep them in the right time line. But for now, I had to get cleaned up. I could see that my stuff was still here. I was especially glad to see that I had some clean clothes. I peeled off the clothes I had been wearing. My shirt could almost stand up on its own. Now I really knew why no one wanted to ride in the same elevator with me. I was definitely ready for that hot shower. That shower seemed to sting a little more than I thought it should, but, after all, it had been a while since I had taken one.

Looking down at the water running off me, I started to wonder what I'd gotten myself into. Not only was the water dirty, it was bloody. That's when I realized that some of the stinging feeling was due to all the cuts and scrapes I had on me. I was beginning to think maybe I'd violated one of those Singapore fines and had been caned as punishment, but these weren't those kinds of marks. They were more like I'd been through a field full of barbs and thistles. If you know Singapore, there's no place there that has barbs and thistles, or anything like them. So where have I been? And how did I get there and back? And, why?

For now, I wasn't going to think about all that. I suddenly realized how hungry I was. I needed to finish getting cleaned up, get dressed, and get something to eat. The Denny's across the street had a big selection, but I really wasn't in the mood for Chinese food. And by the way, the Chinese food at the Denny's in Singapore is real Chinese food. Not like the Americanized version you get in the States.

That left me with a few choices. Fast food places like McDonald's and Burger King were not options, even though there were about 8 of them in walking distance, a local Steakhouse, a few local cuisine restaurants, or the Hard Rock Café down Cuscaden Road, unless I wanted to take a long drive to the East Coast Seafood Village. Seafood sounded really good, but I really wasn't in the mood for a long ride, so I opted for the Hard Rock Café. Nothing like an American style cheeseburger, fries and a drink to try and get my mind back on what had happened to me.

As I climbed the steps to get to the Hard Rock, that feeling about using my credit card came back to me. Should I use it and risk someone, whoever it might be, being able to track me down. Then the hunger pangs started, along with the pain from the scratches and cuts, and I decided I'd have to take the risk. I bypassed the gift shop on the left since I had more T-shirts from here than I needed. Besides, a Singapore large is kind of like an American small. They just don't fit.

I finally made it into the restaurant part and asked for a seat in the corner, instead of a seat in the middle section. I wanted to have my back to the wall so I could see who all came in. I'm not sure who I was looking for, or why, I just wanted to be looking.

As the waitress, a small Singapore girl who looked all of 18, came over, I was trying to decide if wanted to try and dull my senses with a beer, or two, or if I wanted to keep on my toes by drinking a Coke. I decided I'd better keep my senses in check. Never know when that spidey sense might come in handy. I ordered a cheeseburger and fries to go along with it. Might as well order an American meal since I seemed to be the only American in the place.

As I was waiting for my meal, I couldn't help but look around at all the typical Hard Rock Café memorabilia hanging on the walls. Just like every other Hard Rock Café I'd been to, there were guitars, clothes from famous entertainers (some of whom I'd never heard of), and all kinds of posters and song sheets. It reminded me of the Hard Rock Café in London. I had seen a poster there that talked about a concert that was going on where the warmup band was the Beatles. That was probably the most interesting poster I'd ever seen at a Hard Rock. Not too many of those posters around, I suppose.

After I got my food and took my time eating, I used my credit card to pay, even though my spidey sense was still tingling a little. Maybe I was just being paranoid. Anyway, I decided I'd walk back to the Hilton through the Forum shopping center rather than walking around it on the streets. I stopped a few yards from the entrance to wait for a group to go into the Hilton, so I could blend in with them. Just wanted to make it harder in case someone was there waiting for me.

Once again, I got my key and made it to the elevator without a problem. When I got to my room and opened the door, a flood of images hit me like a ton of bricks. It was time to get some rest and try to get those images focused and put some order to them. It had been a long day, or week, I'm not sure, so I laid down on the bed and quickly fell asleep, wondering what tomorrow might bring.

CHAPTER 2

WHAT A NIGHT! I wonder if those were dreams or more of the flashes I'd had before. Or maybe a combination of both. As I started getting ready for the day, I can't help but think about what I'd been through the past few days. The dreams I had last night started to come more into focus. They were the first day or so of what I'd been seeing in the flashes, but they added more detail to them. I guess I never really passed out from that pinch in my neck in front of Lucky Plaza. It seems my alter-ego woke up. I'm beginning to remember walking back through the tunnel and catching an MRT to Changi Airport.

Now, where did I go? I decided to hack into the airport's records to see if I could find out where I had gone. There's another one of those strange things. How and when did I learn how to hack into computer systems? I guess it doesn't matter. I just need to get started so I can start getting my life back in order. At least this life. And to find out what my other life is really like.

It really didn't take long to get into the airport's systems. That's kind of scary. I wonder how many other people have done that. And what they might have done. I decided to keep going in trying to find out where I'd gone, but I was beginning to wonder if maybe those who were in control of my alter-ego had been in the system before and changed my itinerary. Anyway, I had to start looking. Maybe what is in there, true or not, might trigger some more memories, instead of just the flashes and the dreams.

Finding my flight information didn't take long. I flew from Singapore to Manila. Then a flight from Manila to Baguio. The last time I was in Baguio, I was driven there. The Baguio airport gets tends to get fogged in, frequently, so driving there is something that happens a lot, even though the road is not that wide and has a very steep drop on one side, and there isn't much of a guard rail. Pretty much a small curb to try to keep you from driving down a several hundred-foot drop into a valley. Not too bad on the way to Baguio, since going that way we were on the mountain side, not the valley side.

What did I do in Baguio? I really need to get my dreams and flashes to start coming together. I know I didn't go there to play golf at Camp John Hay, although it is an interesting course, especially a hole called Heart Attack Hill. It's so steep, there is a rope tow on the right side to help you get up it. Maybe next time. I decided to go up to the pool on the roof of the Hilton and sit in the sun for a while, thinking it would help me get my mind on track.

I forgot just how hot it is in Singapore. I shouldn't be surprised since it's only about 2 degrees north of the equator. The humidity is also high since it's basically an island. But at least it's a little cooler up on the roof with a slight breeze. I decided to sit under an umbrella instead of out in the sun. It's just too hot.

Sitting there, I allow my thoughts to drift off, thinking my time in Baguio will come into focus. Thinking too hard can suppress memories sometimes. I just need to get a drink, sit back and relax for a while.

CHAPTER 3

I GRABBED A TAXI AT the Baguio Airport and went to Camp John Hay to meet with Major Jonathon Daniels. Major Daniels is responsible for gathering intelligence on several countries in Southeast Asia. After some pleasantries, we got down to business. I asked Major Daniels why I was triggered to come meet with him. "We have learned that there is a major terror threat planned in Taipei that we'd like you to help quell. You need to be there tomorrow and let us know what you find out as soon as you can." "How much time do we have?" I asked. "Our best estimate is that it will happen in the next couple days, so you don't have a lot of time. I know you normally like a little more time, but this is the best we can do." I said, "I'll do what I can. Do you have any contacts I should meet when I get there?" "Unfortunately, right now, you'll have to work on your own. We found out we can't trust any of our normal contacts on this one, but we're working on it."

We discussed a few more operational details while enjoying a few drinks. I only had about an hour until I needed to get back to the airport to get back to Manila and then get a flight to Taipei. I asked my taxi driver to take me on a quick tour of Baguio to see what had been damaged during the earthquake a few years ago. I remember staying at the Radisson Hotel, which was destroyed in the earthquake. I also wanted to see the hill where youngsters stood on the slope to catch coins tossed in the air at them. I was hoping they no longer did such a dangerous thing. Fortunately, there were no kids there doing that. I asked the taxi driver when they stopped. He said it was about 3 years ago when the city banned it, after several boys fell down the hill and were seriously hurt. Feeling good that they stopped, but sad that it took having those kids getting hurt, I asked the driver to take me to the airport.

The hour flight to Manila was uneventful, which is always a good thing. Getting from the Domestic Terminal to the International Terminal took a little longer than I expected. Just a busy afternoon in Manila, I guess. As I walked into the International Terminal, I was approached by a young American who handed me a package with a ticket to Taipei and information about a hotel there. I took the package and headed to the gate. Since I had a couple hours before my flight, I ended up going to the airline's courtesy lounge, since the seat I had was in first class. It was much quieter and the drinks were free. What more could you ask for?

CHAPTER 4

BY THE TIME I got to Taipei, it was getting pretty late in the day. I got a taxi to the Park Taipei Hotel and checked in. I realized I hadn't eaten for a while, so I asked the Concierge where a good restaurant was, within walking distance. Since I'd never stayed in this area of Taipei, I wasn't familiar with where to go. My one other time here, I stayed in an area to the west of downtown and was introduced to Mongolian Bar-B-Que. Surely there was a good place to eat close by.

The Concierge told me about a few places. One of them happened to be an Italian restaurant, which sounded pretty good, so that's what I opted for. As I walked toward the restaurant, another young American started walking along with me and handed me another package. Major Daniels had told me to expect this, so I took the package and continued to the restaurant.

It was good to see that most of the "snake alleys" were gone. Those were places where vendors would hang snakes from a hook, slit them from top to bottom, and collect the blood in a cup for you to drink. This was supposed to be an aphrodisiac or a way to increase your virility. To me it was something strange to look at. I never took part in that, even though I'd participated in a few other "virility" dishes. But those were in Manila, where balut, a boiled, fertilized duck egg is eaten. It was supposedly the way to increase your virility. Once was enough for me. The whole group I was with, including the locals, took part, so I decided it couldn't be that bad. The buddy that was with me at the time might have disagreed. He looked at his duck and wondered if it would crunch when he bit into it. Unfortunately for him, it did. All the beer we'd had before that made it a lot easier to keep it down. But back to Taipei and tonight's dinner.

I continued to find my way to the Italian restaurant, getting a little hungrier as I went. I realized I hadn't eaten all day. I should have asked the taxi driver in Baguio to take me to a restaurant instead of sightseeing. Too late now. As I entered the Botega del Vin, I asked for a table where I could have my back against the wall and could see people as they came in. Seems like I do that a lot lately.

I ordered a glass of wine and my meal, then started looking through the package I'd been handed. Things took a serious turn when the first thing I found was a Glock 9mm. They usually don't give me a weapon. The good thing about Glocks is that they are all black. That makes them easier to hide since there are no shiny parts. This one had a high capacity clip in place, along with two other loaded high capacity clips. That's when my spidey senses really got tingly. Going from not normally having a weapon to getting one with three high capacity clips was a good indicator that this was not going to be an ordinary mission.

Putting the weapon and all the ammo back in the package, and taking a pretty large sip of wine, I started through the intel papers that came out next. It seems there was supposed to be a shipment of nuclear material coming into Taiwan through the Bisha Fishing Harbor near Keelung City in the next day or so. This wasn't weapons grade, but it could be used for a dirty bomb. A dirty bomb, placed in the right location, could cause a lot of the 7 million people living in the area to be killed or suffer radiation sickness. My first thought was, who would want to do this? But that's not my job. I'm sure someone up the line knew who was responsible and why, after all, they were the ones that got me involved. My job was to hunt down the bad guys and keep it from happening.

There's always an incentive to make sure I stop these kinds of things from happening. After all, I'm normally near where ground zero would be if I fail. Makes failure a really bad option. As I look through the manifests and itineraries of all the boats coming into Bisha Fishing Harbor over the next two days, I notice one really gets my spidey senses going. I don't know right now if it's the name of the boat (The Grisham), the name of the captain (Tsei Shin), or something in the manifest. But something there has really got my senses tingling. And no, it's not the same kind of tingling Chris Matthews of MSNBC had a few years ago when Barack Obama was elected President.

Just to be safe, I continued looking through the rest of the boats, crews and manifests expected over the next few days. Only one other boat, The Rockford, got a little bit of tingle going, so I kept it and the big tingle one out to look through in a lot more detail. The good news was, they weren't expected to make it to Bisha until around 1:00 tomorrow afternoon. Interesting thing was, both boats were expected in at about the same time, with the Rockford, a slightly bigger boat, expected in about a half hour before the Grisham.

I could see the waitress coming toward me with my order, so I quickly put everything back in the package and waited for her to put down the plates and pour me another glass of wine. She seemed to be in her mid-twenties, had a wedding ring on and had a look like she has at least one kid, if not two. I looked around the restaurant at the rest of the patrons. Everyone seemed to be having a good time. Drinking, eating, talking and laughing. That's what I always manage to do. Get a good look at who might be hurt if I don't do my job. It's how I get myself really motivated, even more than before, to do what I need to do to stop these kinds of things from happening. And, hopefully, they never know what almost happens or who stops it from happening.

The Botega del Vin turned out to be a good choice. The food was excellent, as was the wine. The waitress, Stella, did an outstanding job and got a really nice tip, even though it's not customary to tip in Taiwan. I told her it was to help with her kids. She told me then that she had two, a son and a daughter, ages 5 and 3, and that it was difficult for her to take care of them the way she wanted. I guess that's a universal problem nowadays. It doesn't matter if you're in Taipei, Tokyo, Trier, or Trenton, taking care of your kids is always a hard job. When she finally looked at how much I'd given her, you could see her eyes start to well up. She thanked me and put the money away, walking a little more gingerly toward the kitchen.

I sat there for a few more minutes before I thought about heading back to the hotel. I scanned the crowd a couple more times, just to see if anyone set of my spidey senses. When no one did, I took the Glock from the package and put it in my right front pocket. I'd need to either get a jacket or wear my shirt untucked so I could carry it where I needed it to be tomorrow.

The night air was cool and had a hint of rain, even though it wasn't raining at the moment. I decided to take a cab back to the hotel. If it smelled like rain, it wouldn't be long before it actually started raining. Taipei had definitely changed since my last visit. It used to be that sewage was dumped in the same drains as rainwater, and those were open drains right below the sidewalks. It made the place have some very interesting odors. It's why I always wanted it to rain while I was here. Rain would clean out the sewage and the smells that went with it. Tonight, though, I didn't care if it rained or not. But if it did, I didn't want to get soaked. So even though it was only a few blocks away, I took the taxi back.

I made my way to my room, took a long hot shower, and sat at the desk for a while, studying the two boats that had got me tingling. There was really nothing in The Rockford's manifest that caught my eye. It was really that there was very little listed that made me worry. For that size boat to not be carrying much cargo was not normal. That must have been what set off my spidey alarm. If they weren't carrying cargo, they must be carrying passengers. And passengers that aren't listed are normally not the kind of people you want coming ashore.

Then there was the Grisham. What was it about it that got me riled up? The captain, Tsei Shin, was nothing out of the ordinary. He'd been a boat captain for nearly 8 years and, according to his file, had been captain of this boat for the past 3. However, the name of the boat was changed to The Grisham about 4 months ago. The captain's name still had me wondering, though. I decided to put him on the back burner and see what else might come up. What was it about the name of the boat that got me going? Why was it changed to the Grisham? Something was really odd. My spidey senses were almost out of control.

Then it hit me. One of John Grisham's first books was titled, "A Time to Kill"! Could it really be that obvious? Are these terrorists that arrogant that they'd name their means of transportation after an author who wrote a book with that title? They want this to be their time to kill nearly 7 million people. I can't let that happen!

CHAPTER 5

WELL, THAT LITTLE REST on the roof of the Hilton was helpful. It's amazing that all those things could have happened in such a short time. My mind was reeling, thinking about the events from Singapore to the Philippines to Taiwan. I'm not sure I want to go back and bring back the rest of those memories. The cuts and scrapes I got somewhere along the way were really starting to ache. Maybe a quick dip in the pool will help ease some of those aches.

After a little longer soak than I planned, I decided it was time to go get something to eat. After I'd gone to my room and cleaned up, I decided to take a walk down Orchard Road and see what was available. There were still the McDonalds' and Burger King's that seemed to be every hundred yards, but fast food just wasn't in the cards. I'd walked down Orchard Road past Lucky Plaza a few times, but that was long ago, and some of the places I remembered weren't there anymore.

I was thinking about the East Coast Seafood Village, but it was too early in the day for that. Besides, I still didn't want to make that long ride, so the Marriott Café in the Tang Plaza Hotel seemed like the best alternative. They have a great selection of seafood, salads, meats and, best of all, desserts. The fact that it is a buffet was just the icing on the cake, which I planned on having at least one piece of before I was done.

I took my normal seat in the corner, facing the door. That seemed to be my norm lately. I always kept my eye on the door. I'm starting to think my spidey sense was protecting me. The whole time I've been recalling what happened since I woke up on Sentosa, my spidey sense has never gone off on something going on around me. Granted, it has gone off several times, but always about those flashes and memories. It has saved me quite a few times.

There was a commercial on TV in the US several years ago where the person said "I can't believe I ate the whole thing!". Well, I can't believe I ate all that! There were the crab legs, the steak, the salmon, the salads, and, of course, the cakes and other desserts. I had thought about stopping by the Haagen-Dazs shop on the way back to the Hilton, but I could barely walk now after all I'd eaten. It reminded me of my college days when I had biochemistry lab on Friday afternoons. Lecture was Friday morning, so a group of us would go to a buffet between lecture and lab. It helped us through the 6 – 8 hours we'd spend in the lab, but for the first hour or so we couldn't sit down. It was great being that young. Now, the walk back to the Hilton is what I'll need to be able to keep functioning.

I needed to get back to those memories. My spidey sense is telling me that I'm not quite finished with what was going on at the Bisha Fishing Harbor in Taiwan. That may be why I'm remembering those things. That's not what normally happens. This is the only mission I've remembered once I "woke up". Either that, or something extraordinary happened there. I've got to get back to where I can remember what went on.

Since the chaise lounge by the pool at the Hilton got me there before, I guess the best thing to do is go back there and try to get in the groove again. Just as I pass the Haagen-Dazs stand, I get one of those spidey sense shivers. Trust me, you normally don't get shivers walking down the street in Singapore. There's something ahead that isn't going to be good.

I decided to make a U-Turn around the Haagen-Dazs stand and see who might start following me. I got to the corner and went into the bookstore at Paterson Road. There were some comfortable chairs there that had a good view of the sidewalk along Orchard Road. I started taking note of every person passing by. The guy in the red shirt and jeans raised a flag. I'm not sure why. My spidey sense didn't go off, but there was just something about him. I'd have to keep an eye out for him. The blonde girl in the white blouse and capris also stood out to me. There was just something about the way she was walking that didn't look right. Just as she passed the entrance walk, I got another one of those shivers. I'll definitely keep an eye out for her.

I sat there for about 20 minutes, watching everyone walking by. The guy in the red shirt walked back by once. I decided he wasn't a threat. The blonde, however, must have walked by at least 6 times. My spidey senses saved me again. I decided to see if she walked by again, away from the Hilton. If she did, I'd make my way back to the Hilton and the sanctuary of my room. I'd been reading, or at least looking like I was, a newspaper, so I was less obvious. Sure enough, the blonde walked back by, heading away from the Hilton. I kept my eye on her as she crossed Paterson Road and headed toward the MRT station.

As soon as she was out of sight, I put down the newspaper and headed for the Hilton. I walked a little faster than I normally do to get there. I learned a long time ago how to walk in Singapore. The first couple of times I was here, I walked like I did back home. I always sweated a lot. I thought it was because of the heat, since like I said before, it's so close to the equator. Then a Singaporean friend of mine clued me in. He said, "Look at how the Singaporeans are walking. They walk a lot slower than all the tourists. That's why they don't sweat as much as guys like you."

But I really didn't care about sweating right now. I needed to get back to the Hilton and the relative safety of my room. It normally took me about 8 minutes to make the trip from Paterson Road to the Hilton. This time I did it in 4. Got in and to my room in less than 3 minutes, and my spidey senses didn't go off once. I guess the nap I had planned by the pool wouldn't happen. I wonder what the blonde had planned for me. I am normally the one who does the hunting, not the one who is hunted. I'll have to figure out a way to get her to make her move without getting myself in trouble.

I really wish I hadn't eaten so much. All that food was really making me drag. I wanted to take a nap and get my thoughts back to Bisha Fishing Harbor and figure out what happened, but I knew I'd have to keep on my toes for a little while. That tingle was still there, just not as intense. I wasn't out of danger yet.

I decided to take the stairs down instead of the elevator. Unfortunately, they led to the parking garage under the main floor, so I had to walk outside again, to get to the lobby. The tingling was a little more intense as I approached the doors, but I was more prepared this time, since now, I'm hunting her. I decided to push the tingling to the limit and see what happens. When you're ready for something, it makes it easier to handle the situation than when you're not.

As I entered the lobby, I saw her sitting in the bar area, with her back to the wall and looking toward the door. Sound familiar? She immediately got up and came my way. As she got closer, I could tell she wasn't there to cause me harm, but seemed intent on wanting to help. As she got next to me, she told me her name was Janine and what she wanted. When she said she had information for me from Major Clark, I was definitely relieved. We went back to the bar table where she'd been sitting. This time, though, it was me who sat with my back to the wall to watch the door.

She started to tell me about what had happened in Taiwan, as if I remembered everything. Before she got too far, I had to tell her that not all of my memories of the past few days had come back. Fortunately, what she had started to tell me matched with what I had remembered. That made me feel pretty good. I told her that I had come to on Sentosa Island yesterday with no memories of the past four days. That I had been at the roof pool this morning and had recalled the first day so far. That I had gone from Singapore to the Philippines to Taiwan and had found out about the Rockford and Grisham coming in the next day. That was as far back as my memory had come.

I knew she knew more about what had happened in Taiwan, but I told her I needed more time to have those memories come back before I let her try to confirm what had happened. I wanted to be sure I knew what really happened before I got a version that might not have been totally true.

With that, we ordered a drink, sat and talked for a while so my huge lunch could settle a little more, then decided to meet again later tonight, here in the bar. Maybe tonight would be my chance to go to the East Coast Seafood Village. That would give us time to talk about the memories that might come back this afternoon.

CHAPTER 6

I DECIDED I'D GO BACK up to the roof pool since it seemed to work so well this morning. As I made my way back to my room to change, I started to get some flashes of the second day in Taipei. I hurried and changed and got to the pool. Then the flashes changed to memories. I let them start really flowing. I'd really like to be able to remember all of what had happened there before I met Janine for our trip for dinner tonight.

The night in Taipei was uneventful. About half way back to the hotel in the taxi, it started raining. I was really glad I'd made the decision to take the taxi. I grabbed my package and made my way to my room. The young guy who had handed me the package on the way to the restaurant was waiting for me in one of the lobby chairs. He had another envelope for me. He quickly handed it to me as I kept walking and he headed out the door.

I got to my room and started going through the rest of the first package and opened the envelope. Needless to say, there would be a lot of studying tonight. It was a good thing I had a photographic memory. Or as Sheldon Cooper would say, an eidetic memory. It makes preparing a whole lot easier.

The rest of the package, which also contained the other two clips to the Glock, had detailed maps of the Taipei area. There were markings that indicated the most likely places a dirty bomb could be set off to inflict the most damage. Each location was marked with wind direction, so I checked the weather forecast to find out which direction the wind would be blowing tomorrow afternoon and for the next two days. Luckily, tomorrow was predicted to have very strong winds to the east. That means that it was highly unlikely they'd try anything tomorrow. No matter where they set it off to the west of the city, strong winds would quickly push everything out to sea before there would be much damage. That was the good news.

The bad news was, the winds would be nearly ideal for an attack the next day with the best place to set off the dirty bomb being near Bisha Fishing Harbor, just a little closer to Taipei. That meant I had tomorrow morning to scout things out on the two locations marked on the map near there, before I started watching for the Rockford and the Grisham coming into the harbor in the afternoon.

As I studied the locations, I saw that one of them could easily be rendered useless for an attack. The satellite photos showed that with only a little effort, I would be able to block, or at least cause any radioactive material to be redirected away from the heart of the city. The second location wasn't going to be as easy.

With the strong winds tomorrow, I knew I had time to see what came off each boat and where things went, before I started making the first site useless to them. Then, I could start checking out the second site more closely to see what I could do there. Being physically there would make it a lot easier to decide what to do and how to do it. I looked again at the map and the predicted wind directions for the next few days and decided there were no other sites on the satellite map that would be useful. Unless, of course, they wanted to wait for about three days. That didn't seem likely. It would be too dangerous to be sitting around with that much nuclear material and have a bunch of people sitting around waiting. It would draw too much attention and increase the chances that one of them would make a mistake and get local officials involved. I knew they didn't want that to happen.

The second site was in a valley off Xiding Road, not far from the Buddhist Temple. The valley would direct the wind directly into the city. It would allow the most radiation to make it into Taipei and cause the most harm. That had to be where I needed to focus my attention.

After reviewing the rest of the potential sites and convincing myself that they weren't viable, I decided to take a shower and get some sleep. Tomorrow was going to be a busy day!

CHAPTER 7

I GOT UP EARLY AND got ready for my adventures for the day. I made my way to the small café at the hotel and had breakfast. My young American friend seemed to have anticipated what I was going to do, and joined me for breakfast. It was the first time we'd actually talked to each other. His name was Joseph Andrews. As we talked, he volunteered to help me with whatever I needed him to do. He seemed to be an intelligent young agent. I wasn't sure how much I could trust him, based on my conversation with Major Clark, but I decided to take my chances with him. After all, my spidey senses have never kicked in with him. It would be good to have a little help, too.

I told him about the first site and what I had planned to do to it to make it useless to the terrorists. I left out the fact that they were planning on detonating a dirty bomb. No use getting him all worked up for nothing. At least for now.

The good news about my new helper was, he had a car and knew how to get around the area. After we finished our breakfast, Joseph left to get his car. He picked me up in front of the hotel and we drove to the first site. When we got there, I noticed some differences between the satellite map and what was there. The satellite photos were only a couple days old, so the changes were kind of unusual. As Joseph and I got closer, I noticed a group of people that didn't seem to belong and began to wonder if maybe the Rockford had already made it to port and these guys were from that boat. Then Joseph told me that he recognized some of them as people he'd been working with the past month or so since he'd been in-country.

We stopped a little short of the site and started paying attention to what they were doing. It looked like they were making the changes to the location that I had planned to make. That was a good thing. It would save me a lot of time. I decided to get out of the car and let Joseph go on to the site and talk to the guys doing the work. No need for them to know I was around.

As Joseph got closer to them, I could see a couple of guys near the entrance, who I hadn't seen before. They looked like they were pretty well armed. They also looked like they recognized Joseph and let him through without even stopping him. When Joseph got to the site where the rest of the people were working, one of them went over to Joseph's car and started talking to him. He looked a little surprised that Joseph had come to this place. They talked for about 10 minutes and then Joseph turned around and left, driving back to where he'd dropped me off.

After a quick pickup, short enough to keep the guys working at the site to not even notice that he'd picked me up, we started to the second site. About halfway there, I asked Joseph to pull over. I wanted to know what was happening at the first site. Joseph explained that those guys had gotten orders from Major Clark to do some work there. They didn't know why. They were just following orders. When I asked Joseph for details of what they were doing, it was amazing that they were doing pretty much what I had planned on doing. That was a relief. They could do it a lot quicker than I could and it left me, and Joseph, to spend more time on the second site.

Getting to the second site near the Buddhist Temple, took about 20 minutes. Not a lot of traffic, just the curving roads in the hills. Some might call them mountains, but since there were trees on top, technically, they're just hills. That's according to my friends in Austria, near the Alps.

After we passed the Buddhist Temple on Shuiyuan Road, we got to the second site. It looked like a small dump site from the satellite map, but it turned out to be what I'd call a squatters' community. This would be an ideal site for the terrorists to hang out, waiting for the wind to shift, since squatters would never get the authorities involved in their community.

Joseph and I ended up driving up the hill to the Observation Deck to get a better view of the valley. The wind was getting pretty strong from the west, just like they said it would, so I knew we had plenty of time before we had to get back to the harbor. I'm sure the strong winds were having an effect on the waves to the east of the island, so I'm sure the terrorists on the boats were getting the rides of their lives. Good for them! It would also delay them from getting into the harbor, so that gave us a little more time to check things out.

As I explained to Joseph what I wanted to do, he offered some suggestions. We then talked about how we were going to get it done before tomorrow. Joseph said he could get the guys from the first site to come over and do most of the work. I hadn't gotten any spidey sense chills when I saw them at the first site, so I agreed. I took some pictures of this site and had Joseph drive me back to the first site. The guys were still there, finishing up the modifications. This time, I went to the site with Joseph and met with the guy he'd talked to before.

It turns out, he was someone I'd worked with before when I was in the region. John, which was the only name I had for him, was by far the best Operative in the region. I was glad to know it was someone I could trust. It was getting close to the time we'd need to get to the harbor to watch the Rockford come in, so Joseph and I asked John to go along with us while his crew finished up here.

On the way to Bisha Fishing Harbor, I filled John in on what was going on. Joseph's eyes got a little big when I mentioned the detonation of a dirty bomb. I asked John if his crew could get over to the second site and start to mingle in with the squatters. They would be there when the terrorists started getting there, assuming that's where they were headed, and start pairing up with them, ready to take them out when needed. If we could take out all of them before they detonated the dirty bomb, it would be a lot easier. And doing it in the squatter community would draw a whole lot less attention.

We got to Bisha Fishing Harbor about 40 minutes before the Rockford was scheduled to come in. I checked for other boats coming in with their posted itinerary and saw that each of the boats coming in so far were about 30 minutes behind schedule. That might give us a little more time, but I didn't want to take any chances. I asked Joseph to park the car so we had a good view of the entrance to the harbor. I gave him first watch, while John and I talked about what we needed to do when we knew for sure where the terrorists were headed.

John agreed to have his crew move to the squatter community. He called the crew leader and told them to get into their "squatter uniforms" and head to the second site. He also told them what to expect in the next few hours. I knew they would be well armed, with both guns and knives. They knew it would be best to keep everything quiet, so knives were the first option. I was glad I may not have to use the Glock, but it was ready just in case.

After about an hour and a half, Joseph, who was on his second watch after John and I took our turns, got excited as he saw the Rockford coming into the harbor. It wasn't as big as I thought it was going to be. As it made its way to a pier, I could see the men on deck looked a little weak-kneed. As the dock crew tied the boat up to the dock, I could see in their faces that they knew the boat's passengers had a rough time.

Most of them looked like seasoned sailors and I knew the rough seas hadn't affected them nearly as much as their passengers.

The passengers finally started to get off the boat and head down the docks toward a large truck. It looked a little like the personnel trucks the military used, where soldiers would all climb in the back, but wasn't as obvious as that. Instead, it had a solid back end, was painted a light blue color and had some writing on the canvas sides. As we all watched them go from the boat to the truck, we could see that they were still suffering from the rough seas they'd just come off of. Again, good for them!

There ended up being 14 of them getting into the truck. We had taken pictures of each of them so John's crew would know who to look for. They might not have that green tint they had right now by the time they got to the squatters' community, but they would all be recognizable. There was one who had gone over to pick up another truck. This one was more of van, than a truck, I guess. The van was likely going to be how they'd transport the nuclear material. That also meant that there wouldn't be many more of them on the Grisham. The van wasn't big enough to carry more than 3 people and the crate the nuclear material was in.

John forwarded all the pictures to his crew. Lucky for us, we had about 30 on our side. They could pair up and target one terrorist each, then switch back and forth keeping an eye on them. John and I finished getting the pictures sent and instructing John's crew on what they needed to do. We just needed to make sure they headed to the squatters' community.

About that time, Joseph let us know that the Grisham had just come into the harbor. It looked a little worse for the wear. It was a smaller boat than the Rockford and probably hadn't done as well during the high winds at sea. I'm sure the terrorists on board made sure their cargo stayed secure, which meant they couldn't have spent much time at the rails when they got seasick. It made me glad I wasn't the one who was going to have to unload that crate.

The Grisham docked closer to where the van was parked. The truck with the 14 terrorists was still in the same spot. I imagine those guys were still trying to get over their seasickness. Another place I'm glad I wasn't. The Grisham crew tied off the boat and helped two people off the boat. A small crane near where they tied up was moved over to lift a crate off the boat onto the pier. A forklift then came to pick it up and took it to the van. That began the comedy of errors we hadn't expected.

It turns out the crate wouldn't fit in the van. No matter how they turned it, the van doors just weren't wide enough. The van driver and the two guys who had accompanied the crate off the Grisham were now in a heated argument. I guess they realized they were making a scene they really didn't want to make, and started talking more quietly. They ended up getting 13 of the seasick guys out of the truck and stuffing them in the back of the van. Since there was normally only room for about 6 in the back of the van, getting 13 in there, who were already seasick, was something to behold. The first 4 or 5 didn't seem to have any problem. It was when the rest of them started squeezing in that things got a little heated.

One of them from the Grisham started taking over, giving directions. That was our clue to who the head terrorist was. We took several pictures of him, along with the second guy from the Grisham, and forwarded them to John's crew. John let his crew know who the lead terrorist was and assigned his best guys to keep track of him. After a few minutes, the lead terrorist, who we ended up naming Bob, decided to only put 8 in the van and the rest in the back of the truck with the crate. The group of terrorists didn't seem too happy about that, so Bob just picked 6 guys and made them get in the truck.

We could see the crate being loaded into the truck now. It had a lot of stains on it, which confirmed that Bob and his buddy from the Grisham spent the whole time at sea watching over their cargo. They couldn't be in really good physical shape right now. It was probably good for them that it was kind of cool out right now. The wind was still strong out of the west, which helped them get over their seasickness faster, it seemed. At least they didn't look as green as they did a few minutes ago. Being stuffed in the van and riding in the truck with the crate of nuclear material along bumpy, winding roads would bring back a lot of that green, I'm sure. At least I hoped it would.

It turns out that John also had an operative working on the dock. During all the confusion with getting the crate from the van to the truck and with all the arguing going on, he had managed to put tracking devices on both vehicles. That meant points in our favor. John checked to make sure he had signals from both tracking devices, which he did. More points in our favor.

The van, with the driver and guys in the back, started heading out of the harbor area. The truck with Bob and his number 2 guy, along with the driver and the guys in the back with the crate, followed the van. With the tracking devices, we decided to wait a few minutes before following. John's operative on the dock was right behind us now in a small red car. We could tell he also was tracking them. I asked John if he was OK driving and if Joseph was OK with letting John drive his car. Then, I had Joseph pull over, let him get with John's operative in the red car and John started driving Joseph's car.

We followed the terrorists to an area east of the city. I guess they realized today would not be a good day to do much more. The area where they stopped was pretty remote. It was also nearly half way between the two sites. We found a hill that overlooked where they were and kept an eye on them for a while. They must have planned for this since they started pulling tents out from under the seats in the truck. I don't think they checked the direction the wind was going to be blowing tonight. Right now, it was strong out of the west. About 9 tonight, it was going to be out of the east. They were setting up their camp to protect themselves from the wind out of the west. They were going to be in for a shocking surprise in about 6 hours.

With a couple of John's guys in place to keep an eye on the camp, John, Joseph and I headed back to the hotel to chill for a while, get something to eat and get ready for tomorrow. We planned on making our way back to the terrorist camp about 4 in the morning. The question was, should we let them start out toward one of the sites in the morning before we started our counter, or try to take them out while they were still at their camp? John checked with his guys monitoring the camp, who reported that the van had left the camp and was heading north. The first site was north of the camp. I'm sure they'll be surprised when they see that what it looks like!

John and I talked about the crate and whether or not it might already be set up and ready to detonate. That would make a difference in our plan. We looked at the pictures we'd taken of the crate while they were trying to figure out how to get it loaded in the van. Typically, if it were set up already, there would be signs of an antenna or an electrical connection that would be used to keep the battery charged during the sea voyage. Fortunately, we had views of each side and the top. None of them had any sign of a way to keep the battery charged. That was a good thing. There wasn't an antenna on any side, either. Again, more points in our favor.

About that time, John got a call from his guy watching the van. Regardless of what Major Daniels said about having help, it sure was nice having John and his crew helping out. It was even good having Joseph around. He was the only one Major Daniels had told me would be able to help.

John's guy reported that the van only spent about 5 minutes at the first site. I guess it didn't take long to figure out that that site wouldn't work for them. It was good that

Bob seemed to be the one casing out the sites. That meant that he wasn't getting any rest after his time at sea. It was about a 30-minute drive on winding roads from there to the second site. Fortunately, the rest of John's crew had already been in the squatters' community for several hours and had started blending in.

We decided that we could take Bob out either in the squatters' community or on the way back to the camp. It would have to look like an accident, though, so timing would be crucial. We had about 20 minutes before Bob made it to the squatters' camp. John told his guys to be ready to put small, remote charges on a couple wheels of the van while Bob and his driver looked around. Knowing the road away from the squatters' community was winding and hilly, it would be easy to have an "accident" on that road.

I asked John to have one of his guys make his way to the tightest hairpin curve on the road with a remote and be ready to set off the charges as the van approached it. We wanted it to keep going off the road and down the hill. We also needed a cell phone jammer in the area to keep Bob from contacting his people if he survived the crash. John got it all set up.

Joseph came up to the table John and I were at and told us that Major Daniels had contacted him and had asked for an update. Joseph put him off for a while so he could ask me what he wanted me to tell him. We decided we'd wait to see how our plan with Bob worked out before we let Joseph report to Major Daniels. After all, it would only be about an hour before we had taken care of Bob. If it all worked out, reporting that Bob was out of the picture should be good news to Major Daniels.

As our dinner was being brought out, John's guy called in to let us know Bob had arrived at the squatters' community. It was good that we had been right about the two sites. I'm not sure what we'd have done if Bob decided to go somewhere else.

One of the advantages of the squatters' community was, when a car, van or truck pulled in, there were several squatters who always converged on it. That would give John's guys even more cover to put the charges in place. On cue, as soon as the van stopped, about 10 squatters came out to greet it. Included with the squatters were three of John's guys. They had talked to the squatters and asked them to make their "visit" to the van a little more eventful than they normally do. They were eager to help. They always ended up getting something from whoever "invaded" their space. This might be an exception, but that would work in our favor. It would cause a little more excitement by the squatters and even more cover for John's guys.

Bob and his driver got out of the van. Bob started walking toward the hill that the Observation Deck was on, through the squatters' homes. That left the driver to guard the van by himself. The squatters converged on the driver's side of the van, causing Bob's driver to take up position there. That let John's guys easily put the charges on the passenger side wheels. I love it when a plan comes together. At least so far.

A few minutes later, Bob came walking back to the van and shooed away the squatters. They weren't too happy that they hadn't gotten anything from Bob and his driver, so they let them know. Bob then tried to explain that they'd be back tomorrow and would bring them all kinds of stuff. That seemed to satisfy the squatters, at least for now. Tomorrow would be different for them. Little did Bob know, today would be different for him. In about 15 minutes.

The driver started out of the squatters' area and headed toward the camp that had been set up. Soon after they had set the charges, John's guys had also headed out of the area and got in position to set off the charges at the hairpin turn with the biggest drop-off. They also had the cell phone jammer set up there, just in case Bob survived the "crash" since he'd have heard the charges go off and knew his mission had been compromised. We didn't want him to tell his crew. We really didn't want him to survive the crash, but had to be ready for every contingency.

One thing about John's guys, they were really good at what they did. Just as the van was approaching the hairpin turn, which the driver was taking a little too fast anyway, they set off the charges. That made the van go straight off the road and down into the valley. The van first went tumbling front over back, then started rolling on its side. There shouldn't be any way that Bob and his driver could survive. Since they'd turned on the cell phone jammer, they couldn't let us know until they'd confirmed Bob had been neutralized. They had actually videoed they whole thing. Including their trek down the hill to confirm Bob's status.

As soon as they reached the wreckage, they were able to confirm that Bob and the driver didn't survive the crash. They also saw that the van was so damaged, it was nearly impossible to see that charges had been put on the wheels. They ended up finding Bob's cell phone and took it with them. Since it was such a remote area, it would be quite a while before the wreck would be reported, if it ever was. Regardless, they managed to get in and out of the wreckage area in less than 10 minutes.

John, Joseph and I were just finishing our dinner when John's phone rang. It was the video of the "crash" that had taken place just minutes before. After he watched it, he handed his phone to me so Joseph and I could also see what had happened. I'm not one who relishes killing others, but in this case, with so much on the line for so many people, I knew it was something that had to have been done. We knew this would delay their plans. There didn't seem to be a good second-in-command that we had seen in any of our surveillance.

We sent Joseph off to meet with John's guys and retrieve Bob's cell phone. That left John and I to come up with our own plan of attack, now that Bob was out of the game. John contacted the guys who were watching the camp to see if anything had changed there. The terrorists had continued to make camp, expecting the strong wind to stay out of the west. They set up their campfires a few feet to the east of their tents. The tents blocked the wind, for now, and they started making their dinner. It wouldn't be nearly as good as what John, Joseph, and I had just had. Too bad for them.

When the terrorists had finished their meal, some of them started to head toward the road where Bob should have been coming from. John's guys were a little too far away to see their faces, but they could tell the terrorists were beginning to get a little worried. Based on when Bob had left the squatters' area, he should have been back to the camp about a half hour ago. We knew he wasn't going to make it on time. The terrorists didn't. After another half hour, the terrorists started gathering at the camp. By now I'm sure they knew something had happened to Bob. They just didn't know what.

It looked like they were going to go try and find Bob, but they had two major problems. The only other vehicle they had was the truck with the crate, which I'm sure they didn't want to drive around in, and the wind was starting to change direction, blowing the campfire smoke directly into their tents. They must have decided that Bob could take care of himself because they started tearing down the tents and moving them so they weren't being filled with smoke. Either way, they wouldn't be getting a good night's sleep. No Bob to tell them what to do and tents that would take days to air out.

After John's guys overseeing the camp finished their report, we decided we could relax for a while. Joseph had returned with Bob's cell phone, John decided to head back to his place, Joseph had to go make his report to Major Daniels and I decided to go to my room and check out the contacts on Bob's phone. We decided to meet at 6:00 the next morning to put our plan into motion.

CHAPTER 8

I HAD SPENT A COUPLE hours after Joseph and John left last night going through Bob's phone contacts and call records. There was one number that Bob had made several calls to. Interestingly enough, it was a number in the United States. Half the calls were incoming, so whoever it was that made those calls to Bob could have been his handler. That got me a little worried. Enough that my spidey senses started tingling just a little. Not enough to get worried about, but enough to make a note of it.

John and Joseph were right on time. We each grabbed something off the Continental breakfast bar and headed out. Today was the day we'd have to take care of whatever was in the crate. Getting to the terrorist camp without an incident wouldn't be easy. John's over-watch guys had told John that the terrorists had been restless all night since Bob hadn't gotten back and it looked like it was hard for them to sleep in their smoke-filled tents. There still didn't seem to be anyone who was taking charge, which was fine with us.

Joseph let us know that Major Daniels liked what we'd done the day before with Bob and his driver. He pretty much gave us the green light to do whatever we felt we needed to do. That was a good thing, since that's what we were going to do anyway.

On the way to meet with John's over-watch guys, John and I decided that we'd have to see the actual layout of the terrorists' camp before we could finalize our plans. The stakes were just too high. If we didn't execute our plan precisely, there was a chance that one of the terrorists knew how to detonate the dirty bomb. That wasn't a chance we were willing to take.

We finally met up with John's over-watch guys. Getting there was a little tougher than I'd imagined. We'd had to make our way through some thick brush that had barbed plants that put some pretty good cuts on our legs. As we approached John's guys, we had to crawl the last 20 feet so the terrorists couldn't see us. Now the plants were cutting into our backs as well. I couldn't complain, I guess. John's guys had done the same thing yesterday and had spent the night up here while I had been in my hotel room.

The over-watch location was the perfect place to see what was going on in the camp. John's guys let us know that 3 of the terrorists had taken off after they'd gotten their tents moved around. They had walked down the path to the road. After they'd been gone for about 20 minutes, one of them came back to the camp and started directing the others. This guy we named Bob 2. The other two who had left the camp were gone for several hours. They had come walking back into the camp at about 3 in the morning.

Since we still had guys watching the crash site, we knew that those two hadn't found it. Nor had anyone else. The longer no one found it, the better. But today was another day, and the crash site might be visible from the Observation Deck above the squatters' area. John had a couple of his guys go to the Observation Deck to check it out. We'd find out if the van could be seen from there in about 20 minutes. The Observation Deck wasn't the most popular destination, so, even if the van were visible, there was a good chance there wouldn't be anyone there to see it today.

The camp started to become a little more active as the sun started warming things up, rising over the hills to the east. We asked John's guys which of the terrorists was Bob 2. It turns out he was the short, heavy set one. Not one you would normally expect to be the leader of the group. I guess I shouldn't have jumped to that conclusion. After all, Khalid Sheikh Mohammed, the mastermind of the 9/11 attacks in 2001 was short and heavy set. At least he was when he was captured.

John and I decided that we needed to try and capture Bob 2. He had probably been the leader the whole time. He had just let Bob look like he was the leader to keep himself safe. That was a typical tactic with terrorists. Let someone else take the first bullet. Since Bob hadn't come back, Bob 2 decided he had to expose himself as the leader. With Bob and the van driver gone, that only left 14, including Bob 2, to try and finish their mission.

One thing the terrorists had done right was picking their campsite. Even though they didn't do well with setting up their camp, the location was a good one. There was no way for us to get into it without being seen. Even the path from the road could be easily seen from the camp. That meant there was no way to make a direct attack on the camp.

There's a saying that says "Fortune favors the Prepared" or "Fortune favors the Bold". I'm not sure how prepared we were, but I felt pretty good about our plan. No matter, we were going to be bold, so we felt fortune was in our favor no matter what. We just had to get all of John's guys up-to-speed on that plan. We left the two over-watch guys in place and made our way, getting even more scrapes and scratches, to a place to meet the rest of John's team.

Sometimes, it doesn't matter how prepared you are, how good your plan is, or how bold you are. This was one of those times. It turns out I'd forgotten to check the weather forecast for the day. Today was not going to be a good day for the terrorists. I'd done a good job checking on how the wind was going to be blowing, but I hadn't paid much attention to how much rain there'd be. Turns out, it was going to be a lot! And it was just starting. It kind of made me feel a little sorry for the terrorists in their tents. Not really!

John, Joseph and I met up with John's crew in a small warehouse about 2 miles from the terrorist camp. The rain gave us some new options. Bob 2 would likely be staying in the truck with the crate. After all, it was probably drier than any of the tents would have been and it hadn't been filled with smoke the night before. He would likely be the only one with a way to detonate the dirty bomb, now that Bob was out of the picture. He would also want to be sure to be able to be close in case something came up. I'm sure he is a little leery now that Bob has disappeared.

CHAPTER 9

WHAT THE..? WAIT A minute! How are my legs getting wet? We're in the warehouse! Oh, never mind. It's one of those monsoon-type showers that pop up in Singapore that woke me from my sleep on the roof of the Hilton. And it was just getting interesting. I guess it'll have to wait now, since I have about 20 minutes to get ready to meet Janine and head to the East Coast Food Village. I wish I'd remembered the whole mission so I could debrief with Janine, but that'll now have to wait. I can fill her in on what I remember so far. The rest will just have to wait until I have a chance to get back to where I can remember the rest.

Janine was waiting for me in the lobby bar of the Hilton, drinking a glass of wine. I was only a couple minutes late. As I came around the corner toward her, she finished off the wine and came to meet me. We went out the front door and the bellman waived for a taxi. The drive to the East Coast Food Village would take about 20 minutes, depending on traffic. Since I really didn't want to get into a discussion about the mission with the taxi driver being able to hear us, we ended up talking about the weather and what she'd been up to that day.

Most people who stay in the Orchard Road area end up shopping at one of the shopping centers, like Lucky Plaza. It turns out, Janine is not a big shopper. While she did spend some time at Lucky Plaza, it was mainly to kill time rather than actually shop for something. Like me, though, she ended up buying something she really didn't need, like another suitcase. I don't know what it is about those suitcases. They just seem to jump out at you and say "Buy me!". I always thought it was just me, but Janine proved me wrong.

Once we got to the East Coast Food Village, we decided to start at the East Coast BBQ Seafood restaurant. After all, I really wanted seafood. We ended up getting seated so I had my back to the corner and could easily see the door. Some habits are just too hard to break. With the chance of more rain showers, we decided to stay indoors instead of eating outside. Besides, with the rain came even higher humidity, so the air conditioning felt pretty good.

We ended up getting an order of Drunken Prawn. If you've never had that, it's quite an experience. Basically, you get a large glass bowl with about 20 prawn in it that are jumping around. The server then pours in Saki and you can see the prawn slowing down as they get drunk on the Saki. Then they take the bowl into the kitchen, where they light up the alcohol in the Saki, cooking the prawn from the inside and outside. They used to do that at the table, but it seems more humane to take them back into the kitchen where you can't see them being cooked alive. When all the alcohol is burned off, they bring the bowl back to the table, where you can reach in, grab a prawn, peel off everything but the tail and eat the tail. It's very fresh seafood.

While we were waiting on the Drunken Prawn, I started filling Janine in on what I had remembered so far. From my trip to the Philippines and then to Taiwan. My report was interrupted several times as different servers came by to either bring food or drinks.

Another advantage of sitting in the corner, you can see servers coming to your table and can stop talking well before they get there.

Given that I was telling Janine about what we'd done with a dirty bomb in Taipei, it would not be a good thing to be talking about in front of a server. Just hearing the words "dirty bomb" might send them into a panic. We really didn't want that to happen in Singapore.

After our meal and reporting on most of the events I'd remembered so far, we decided to walk over to a Hawker Stall called 245 Beer Place's Cold Drinks to have a drink and finish the debrief. Since it hadn't rained any more since we'd gotten there, we decided sitting outside would be OK. It had cooled off a little since the sun had set and the humidity seemed to have gone down a little, too. Don't get me wrong, it was still hot and still humid, but at least it was bearable now.

I finished telling her about the meeting in the warehouse and getting ready to execute our plan. She confirmed everything I'd told her so far. When she started to tell me what happened next, I had to stop her. Again, I wanted to make sure my memories weren't tainted with what someone might tell me. So, we finished our drinks and were on our way to the taxi stand. I hadn't had satay for a while, so we ended up stopping at the Haron Satay hawker stand for a couple skewers of mixed meat satay. We slowly walked to the taxi stand with our satay, talking about the different times we'd been to different places in Asia. We timed our walking and eating satay pretty well, getting to the taxi stand just as we finished the last of the satay.

On the ride back to the Hilton, we talked more about our times in Asia and Europe. While I don't normally remember these debrief sessions, as we talked about the different places and the times each of us were there, more of them started to come to me. When I asked Janine about how many times we had met to debrief missions, she became very quiet. Finally, she started to tell me that this was about the 30th time she had met with me after a mission. She also told me that she knew I had been on at least 30 others that she wasn't involved with.

Needless to say, that was quite a shock to me. I had no memory of any of the missions prior to this one. That was, until that moment. I started to get a lot of memory flashes, like the ones I'd had shortly after I'd come to on Sentosa Island. Janine could tell that I was having those flashes. I think the pinpoint pupils and rapid blinking might have been a clue. She let me get through them, and when she saw my eyes were getting back to normal, she grabbed my arm and brought me back to today.

When I was finally able to talk again, I asked her what had happened to me and how I could have done all of those things without remembering. Since we were about to pull into the Hilton, she told me to wait until we could have somewhere private to talk. Since it was likely that the bar area in the Hilton was bugged, she suggested we walk down to the Haagen-Dazs stand. We each got some ice cream in a cup and sat down on a bench not far from there.

As we sat there, eating our ice cream, she told me about a chip that had been inserted in my head several years ago. It was how I was called to missions. That explained what happened to me a few days ago as I was walking into Lucky Plaza. It was how I went from being mild mannered Larry Walker to becoming Justin Hunter in an instant. She told me how, when a mission was completed, the agency was able to trigger the device to convert me back to Larry Walker and separate Justin Hunter's memories from Larry's. This was the first time that trigger hadn't worked, and Larry's and Justin's memories were merging together.

We decided that I needed to finish my recall of what happened in Taipei. I knew it involved a lot of nuclear material, a potential for two large groups getting into a battle, and me having a 9mm Glock with a lot of ammo that I normally wouldn't have had. Since it was getting late anyway, and my mind was still reeling, I guess going to bed would be a good idea.

CHAPTER 10

IT WAS STILL RAINING outside the warehouse as we finished up our plans on how to deal with the terrorists. I'm sure they are in a pretty foul mood about now. Those tents probably haven't been keeping much rain and wind out. And I'm sure they still have a lot of smoke smell in them, too. Just can't feel sorry for them, though.

The overlook guys let us know that there was only one lookout, that Bob 2 was still in the back of the truck and the rest were in the tents. Since the only thing they found on Bob was a cell phone, we assumed they had a cell phone hooked up to the dirty bomb in order to detonate it. The cell phone jammer had a range of about 300 yards, so getting it within that distance from the truck was crucial. We sent two snipers up to the overlook position, along with their spotters, to help protect John's team and I as we made our move onto the terrorist's position. John had one more thing for me, a silencer for my Glock, which I quickly put on, along with checking that I had the two extra mags of ammo.

John told me two of his guys were pretty Ninja-like, so we decided to have them take the cell phone jammer and get as close to the truck as possible. The rest of us would first eliminate the lookout as quietly as possible, which should be very easy in the heavy rain, then move into the camp. When the snipers were in place, we'd make our move.

It took about 20 minutes for the snipers to get in place and report back. The rest of us had moved from the warehouse and were in position to eliminate the lookout. On my cue, we moved. John's ninjas started toward the truck, John and I moved toward the lookout, and the rest of John's guys got ready to move into the camp.

John and I got to the lookout within a couple minutes. We came at him from the same direction the rain was being blown, so he was facing away from us. One shot took care of him. I don't like taking people out, but in this case, with 7 million people's lives on the line, I had no regrets. I saw the ninjas getting close to the truck, which meant the jammer should be functioning. The rest of John's guys had started moving toward the camp. John and I moved toward the truck. We had to take Bob 2 alive if we could.

As soon as John's guys got in place at each tent and John and I got to the truck, I gave the signal to move. All of the terrorists were eliminated within 10 seconds. John's guys were very good at their jobs. Bob 2 must have heard something because he poked his head out of the back of the truck. As soon as he did, John grabbed him and pulled him out. I could see him reaching for his cell phone, so I shot him in his right arm. No need to take any chances. John grabbed Bob 2's cell phone. I got Bob 2's arms behind his back and John put zip ties on him. We left him facing up, looking into the heavy rain. Not quite water boarding, but close.

As Bob 2 laid there looking into the rain, sputtering, John and I started asking questions. Of course, the first thing we did was let him know that all of his men had been eliminated. We let him look toward his camp so he could see all of John's guys walking toward us. You could see a look of defeat in his face. Then, he was back to looking straight up at the rain, sputtering.

After several minutes of questioning Bob 2, John and I agreed that what Bob 2 told us about the crate, that there were no booby traps, was true. Regardless, we decided to call in a few Marine units to handle the removal of the crate and take care of the nuclear material. Oh, and to remove all signs of the terrorist camp and terrorists, including the van containing Bob and his driver.

About an hour later, three Marine helicopters, flying low over the hills, slipped into the terrorist camp location. As they landed, I see Major Daniels jump out and look around. When he finally sees John and I, a big smile comes over his face. The Marines get quickly to work removing the bodies of the terrorists and tearing down their tents. Another group of Marines moves toward the truck and start working on the crate. After a few minutes working in the truck, the Marines get out, rip off the top of the truck and look to the east. About that time, a heavy lift helicopter makes its way over the hilltop toward the valley.

With the sun starting to set, all signs of the terrorist camp are gone. As usual, the Marines did an outstanding job. Major Daniels, John, Joseph and I made our way back to the warehouse to go over everything that had happened. Major Daniels assured us that the van with Bob and his driver had been removed, too.

It's another case of 7 million people not knowing how close they came to dying. But that's what we do! We operate in the dark, keeping people safe. After about an hour of quickly filling Major Daniels in, everything went blank, just like when I was heading into Lucky Plaza in Singapore. The only thing that came back to me after that were short flashes of being in the back seat of an F/A 18 Hornet.

CHAPTER 11

THAT MUST BE HOW I got back to Singapore so quickly, and still so dirty. So, now I'm back to meeting with Janine to finish my debriefing. The question is, am I going to be Larry or Justin? I guess if I know enough to ask that question, it'll be Justin.

I ended up calling Janine to meet me for breakfast so we could finish the debrief. I finally got to sleep peacefully for a couple hours before I had to get up to meet her. It was the best I'd felt since waking up on Sentosa Island.

As I got to the lobby, Janine was there waiting for me. We opted for a taxi ride to Cedele at the Carlton Hotel in the Downtown Core area. It was time for a little celebration. The talk on the way to the restaurant was cordial. When we got to our table, yep, same seating arrangement, we really started talking about the last day of my time in Taiwan. After I told Janine about that afternoon and evening, she confirmed everything that had happened.

Now I had to figure out how my Larry/Justin alter-egos managed to find each other. Janine was definitely going to have to help me through all that. I haven't had time to process all of my previous missions so she will have to go through the 30 or so that she'd helped me with in the past. By doing that, all the previous missions should come back to me as well. But for now, I wanted to know what happened after I blacked out in Taiwan.

Turns out I was put in the back seat of an F/A 18 Hornet to get me back to Singapore as quickly as possible. We landed on a carrier off the coast of Singapore, then put on a helicopter and dropped off on Sentosa Island. The rest you know, except for what happened to Bob 2 and who was behind the whole issue. Janine and I spent the next couple hours talking about that. Bob 2 was taken to a military base in Guam, where he could be questioned without a lot of the normal rules having to be followed. They were still chasing down the person behind the phone number we found on Bob's phone. Who knows, that may be my next mission, but I normally don't operate on US soil.

So why did my implant not keep Larry and Justin separated? According to Janine, the F/A 18 landing on the carrier was a little dicey. Since I wasn't fully awake when it landed, I got a little more of a jolt than normal, which caused an issue with the chip. Now, I get to process all my other missions. Someday, I may even get to talk about them. Until then, I'm sure I'll have a new mission in the next few weeks. Seems like the bad guys never rest.

Until then, I'll head to Seoul, Korea, to do a little R&R. I remember my first trip to Seoul. Normally, when you exit a plane, you can smell the jet fuel exhaust as you walk up the jetway. Then, I remember the smell of garlic. That's changed over the years as the country has modernized.

There are a lot of things to keep me occupied there. There are also a lot of good things to eat there. One of my favorites is Bulgogi. It's small strips of beef that you cook yourself on a grill in the middle of the table. You can add cloves of garlic, but I normally end up tasting garlic for several days afterward, so I usually don't add them. Once your beef is ready, you take a leaf of lettuce, put some sauce on it, add the beef, make it into a ball and eat it. It is great.

Of course, you can't just have Bulgogi. You have to have the staple that goes with most meals in Korea. Kimchi. There are various forms of Kimchi. Basically, it's cabbage with an assortment of herbs and spices. Depending how long it's left to ferment, it can be crunchy or mushy. I prefer the crunchier version.

Of course, there's a place to go look for suitcases, my Achilles Heel. They are on Itaewon Street. There are all kinds of places to shop, for all kinds of things. In addition to suitcases, there are places to get things from tennis shoes to custom-made suits. There is an ice cream shop, and, of course, several bars. It should be a good time, even if I am by myself.

CPSIA information can be obtained
at www.ICGtesting.com
Printed in the USA
LVHW090910310520
656806LV00010BA/156/J